ThunderTrucks! is published by Stone Arch Books
a Capstone imprint
1710 Roe Crest Drive
North Mankato, Minnesota 56003
www.mycapstone.com

Cataloging-in-Publication Data is available on the
Library of Congress website.

ISBN: 978-1-4965-6492-4 (library hardcover)
ISBN: 978-1-4965-6496-2 (eBook)

Summary: Atalanta is the fastest truck in the world,
and she is out to prove it. It's not going to be easy with
every hero and monster truck challenging her for the
title. And with each race she wins, her challengers get
more devious in their attempts to stop her.

Designed by Brann Garvey

Printed in the United States of America
PA017

THUNDERTRUCKS!

SPEED DASH

BY BLAKE HOENA
ILLUSTRATED BY FERN CANO

STONE ARCH BOOKS
a capstone imprint

CONTENTS

CHAPTER ONE

SUPER SPRINT

"Racers, get ready!" a race official blares.

Atalanta rolls up to the starting line.

She revs her engine.

VROOM! VROOM!

To her right is the mighty Hercules. His engine roars.

RRRR! RRRR!

On her left is Perseus with his winged-shaped mud flaps. His engine rumbles.

RUMBLE! RUMBLE!

There are other ThunderTrucks as well. Theseus, B-phon, Argonutz, and Odysseus all roll up to the starting line together.

Each of them has a special skill. Hercules is the World's Mightiest Truck. He even has a decal that says so. At the ThunderJam 3000, Perseus jumped over

an amazing 90 flaming tires. Theseus is the only ThunderTruck smart enough to solve the Monster Maze.

Atalanta has a special skill too. She is the speediest of them all. At least that is what she hopes to prove at the ThunderTruck Super Sprint.

"Get set!" the official blares.

Engines rev, roar, and rumble even louder.

VROOM! RRRR! RUMBLE!

"GO!" the official blares.

Tires spin. Dust flies. The crowd *HONKS!* and *BEEPS!* as the race begins.

Atalanta zips into the lead. The mighty Hercules quickly falls behind. Even Theseus, Argonutz, and Odysseus cannot keep up. They are all left in Atalanta's dust.

As the racers round a turn, Perseus zooms up a small hill. He leaps high into the air. He lands with a **THUD** next to Atalanta.

"You really are fast," Perseus says with a gasp. He tries to keep pace.

"You haven't seen anything yet!" Atalanta beeps.

Her tires **SQUEAL**, and she darts ahead of Perseus.

B-phon opens his doors. They spread
out wide like wings. WHOOSH!
He takes flight and soars into the air.

Atalanta looks up as he starts to
catch her.

"You won't pass
me," Atalanta beeps.

Her engine whines.
She dashes ahead of
B-phon.

Atalanta darts around the track faster
than any other ThunderTruck. She sails
over jumps and zips around turns. She
zooms down the straightaways.

Up ahead, the official waves a

checkered flag. Atalanta speeds across

the finish line and **SCREEEECHES**

to a stop.

The crowd cheers, "Atalanta! Atalanta!"

The other trucks pass the finish line.

"Wow!" Perseus beeps.

"You are super

speedy," Theseus says.

"I bet we can find you a sticker

that says

'World's Speediest

Truck,'" Hercules adds.

"I bet she's not," a loud voice says.

Suddenly, the crowd goes silent.

A giant, flame-red truck rolls up to the group of ThunderTrucks.

"Bullistic!" the audience gasps.

The MonsterTruck lets out a cloud of smoke.

"You aren't the World's Speediest Truck until you beat me," Bullistic booms.

"I am not afraid to race you," Atalanta says.

"Then I challenge you to a race through the Monster Maze!" Bullistic bellows.

CHAPTER 2

MONSTER MAZE

The next day, Atalanta meets Theseus before the race. He is the only ThunderTruck to ever beat Bullistic.

The Monster Maze is a course full of twists and turns through a dark canyon.

"I brought this to help you," Theseus says.

He sets down a silver winch.

"What's that for?" Atalanta beeps.

"I used it to find my way out of the maze," Theseus says. "Before you enter, hook the cable to a tree near the entrance."

Atalanta puts the winch on her back bumper. She hooks its cable to the tree. Then she goes to face Bullistic.

"The rules are simple," a race official says. "First one to the center of the maze and back wins."

"Got it," Atalanta beeps.

"Racers, get ready," the official blares. Atalanta revs her engine.

VROOM! VROOM!

"Get set!" the official yells.

SNNNOOORRRTTT! Bullistic zooms

off into the maze before the official

even says go!

Atalanta races after him. The cable from the winch trails behind her.

Within the maze, rocky walls tower over her. They block out all but a sliver of sunlight. Soon, Atalanta is lost in the twisting and winding of the tunnels.

"Ugh! Another dead end!" Atalanta honks.

She speeds down a canyon and wheels around a turn. She screeches to a halt as she come grill-to-grill with a rocky wall.

"Again!" she honks.

Twist after turn, Atalanta makes her way through the maze.

The narrow path she raced down opens up into a large cavern. Ahead, the road suddenly disappears. Atalanta **SCREECHES** to a stop at the edge of a cliff.

"Whoa! That was close," she beeps.

Below are sharp, jagged rocks. Atalanta also sees junked trucks at the bottom of the pit.

Then a large, dark shadow moves over her. She spins around to see Bullistic blocking the path.

"Congrats," he snorts. "You have found the middle of the maze."

"Now I just need to find the exit," Atalanta beeps.

"Not going to happen," Bullistic snorts. "You're about to join the rest of my competitors in the pit."

Bullistic's engine roars. **RRRR! RRRR!** His tires **SQUEAL!** as he charges. Atalanta winds the winch's cable around a rock.

When Bullistic leaps forward, she darts to the side. The giant truck trips over the cable.

"AHHHHH!" he screams as he falls into the pit.

BOOM! He lands with a crash.

"Ow! My axle!" Bullistic groans.

"Time to go!" Atalanta beeps.

She follows the cable. She darts down tunnels until she reaches the entrance.

"Atalanta, you did it!" Theseus honks.

"You are the World's Speediest Truck!" Perseus honks.

Just then, a run down gas-guzzler sputters up to them.

"Medusa!" Atalanta beeps. "What do you want?"

"You aren't the World's Speediest Truck until you beat me," Medusa rattles. "I challenge you to a race in the Endur-X Championship."

CHAPTER 3

ENDUR-X CHAMPIONSHIP

The next day, Atalanta meets Perseus at the Endur-X course. He is the only ThunderTruck to beat Medusa.

With just a bump, Medusa can turn any truck into a pile of scrap.

"You also need to be careful of her sisters, the Gorgonaters," Perseus warns. "They will try to cheat to help Medusa win."

"Where are they?" Atalanta asks.

Perseus looks up to the sky.

"I don't know, but I know that

they can fly."

"Racers, get ready!"

the race official yells.

Atalanta rolls up to the starting

line. She stays far away from Medusa.

"Get set!" the official says.

Atalanta revs her engine.

VROOM! VROOM!

Medusa sputters.

"GO!" the official yells.

Atalanta speeds away.

Atalanta looks back as she reaches the first part of the race, Mount Trolympus. She has left Medusa in her dust.

She starts her climb through a narrow canyon. Near the top, a large shadow crosses Atalanta's path.

She looks up just in time to see a boulder dropping from the sky.

SCRRREEECCCHHH! She stops.

BOOM! The large rock crashes right in front of her.

"It must be the Gorgonaters," Atalanta rumbles.

She continues up and over the mountain. On the other side is the Bottomless Bog.

Atalanta sets off slowly down a narrow and twisting path. She does not want to slip off and fall into the bubbling, oily bog.

As she zigs and zags down the trail, another shadow passes over her.

She looks up to see the Gorgonaters. They are carrying Medusa over the bog.

They set their sister down at the end of the path.

Atalanta's way is blocked, but she

is not going to let that stop her. She

revs her engine to build up speed.

VROOM! VROOM!

Then she turns off the path. She

is racing so fast, she skips across the

surface of the oily bog.

The Gorgonaters swoop down to stop her.

"We've got you now!" they scream.

Atalanta spins in a full circle and sprays bubbling oil everywhere. It splatters the Gorgonaters, and they crash into the bog. **SPLISH! SPLASH!**

Atalanta races on. She zooms across an endless desert, jumping over dunes and kicking up sand. She leaves Medusa, chugging and sputtering, far behind her.

She races until the ground drops away on both sides of the path. The thinning path leads to a narrow point.

Atalanta rolls up to the edge of a steep cliff. This is the end of the world!

"I made it!" Atalanta honks.

Then she zips back across the endless desert. She winds her way through the Bottomless Bog. She races up and over Mount Trolympus.

The ThunderTrucks wait for her on the other side.

"You did it!" Argonutz blares.

"You won another race!" B-phon honks.

As they are celebrating, three tough-looking trucks roll up to them.

It is the evil Chimera Brothers.

"She is not the World's Speediest Truck," The Goat bleats.

"Not unless she can beat us!" The Lion roars.

"On our Colossal Course!" The Dragon bellows as flames shoot out from is grill.

CHAPTER 4

COLOSSAL COURSE

The next day, Atalanta meets B-phon at the course. He is the only ThunderTruck to beat the Chimera Brothers.

The Colossal Course is the scariest course yet. It is filled with mud pits to sky-high jumps and steep berms.

"The Chimera Brothers will team up on you," B-phon warns. "First, The Lion will pop your tires with his spiked bumpers.

Then, The Goat will ram you, to knock you over. That's when The Dragon will fry you with his fire."

"Okay, got it," Atalanta beeps.

She rolls up to the starting line with the three MonsterTrucks.

"Racers, get ready!" the official blares.

Atalanta revs her engine.

VROOM! VROOM!

"Get set!"

The Chimera Brothers' engines roar and rumble. **RRRR! RUMBLE!**

"Go!"

Tires spin, and the racers are off.

The Dragon shoots a blast of fire from his grill. Atalanta zigs to the right. The Goat turns to ram into her. Atalanta zags to the left.

The Lion nips at her heels. Atalanta puts the pedal to the metal and she speeds ahead.

Atalanta zips around a turn. She hits a jump and sails over a pile of wrecks. She dives through mud pits and speeds down straightaways.

She is winning! But the Chimera Brothers are not really racing. They are waiting for Atalanta to come around and lap them.

First, she zigs around The Dragon. He tries to blast her with fire.

Next, she zags around The Goat. He attempts to ram her.

Then, she darts past The Lion. He nips at her tires.

"This isn't working!" The Dragon bellows.

"She's too fast," The Lion roars.

"It is Super Monster time!" The Goat bleats.

Atalanta looks back. What she sees causes her to race faster.

As they race, the Chimera Brothers ram into one other. Their parts jumble together until the three MonsterTrucks become one Super MonsterTruck.

"B-phon didn't warn me about this," Atalanta gasps.

The Super MonsterTruck is huge. It has spiked bumpers like The Lion. It has ramming horns like The Goat and a flaming grill like The Dragon. It is now twice as fast and catching up to Atalanta.

"If ever I needed to be the speediest truck in the world," Atalanta beeps, "it is right now."

Blasts of fire melt her mud flaps. Spiked bumpers nip at her tires.

When she comes to an obstacle, she jumps over them. The Super MonsterTruck barrels through them.

Atalanta realizes that the Super MonsterTruck is more interested in smashing her than winning the race.

She slams on her brakes. The Super MonsterTruck speeds by her and skids to a halt.

"You're about to be scrap!" the huge beast roars.

Then it charges, tires spinning and engines roaring. Behind the Super MonsterTruck is the finish line. Atalanta just needs to get by it to win.

The Super MonsterTruck expects her to zig and zag. So Atalanta does something different.

She drives straight at the charging truck! She is small enough to zip right under its axles and finish the race.

CHAPTER 5

MONSTERTRUCK SPEED DASH

The ThunderTrucks gather around to celebrate. Atalanta just won another race! But they are not the only trucks waiting for her at the finish line.

She sees The Boar and the even bigger Atlas. The nine-wheeled Hydra is there, and so is the Cyclops with his one huge headlight.

They are all there to challenge her to a race.

"Enough is enough!" Atalanta honks. "One last race. First one to Royal Rumbler's Decal Shop is the world speediest truck. Agreed?"

The MonsterTrucks all agree.

"Okay then, to the starting line!" she honks.

The MonsterTrucks all do as she says.

"Racers, get ready!" the race official

blares

Atalanta revs her engine.

VROOM! VROOM!

"Get set!"

All the MonsterTrucks rumble and roar.

RUMBLE! RRRR!

"GO!"

Tires spin. Dirt flies. The racers are off!

Atalanta brakes as The Boar veers

left to smash into her. At the same time,

Atlas steers right to ram her. The two

MonsterTrucks crash into each other.

BANG!

Up ahead is Hydra, rumbling along on his nine tires. She zips by him as he tries to run her off the road. Hydra spins out.

Then it is just her and the Cyclops. He swerves all over to block her. But Atalanta is too fast. She darts around him. Cyclops turns too sharply and flips over.

Atalanta zooms off.

A little while later, she rolls into the Royal Rumbler's Decal Shop.

"Can I help you?" the Royal Rumbler asks.

Up on the wall is a decal that says "World Speediest Truck."

"I would like that one," Atalanta beeps.

Then she goes outside as all the other trucks show up.

"I was the fastest at the ThunderTruck Super Sprint," Atalanta blares. "I beat Bullistic through the Monster Maze. I won the Endur-X Championship. And I survived the Colossal Course!"

She pauses and beams her brights at the trucks in front of her.

"Are there any other challengers?" Atalanta rumbles.

The MonsterTrucks all turn and sputter away.

Then the ThunderTrucks gather around to congratulate her.

"You are the World's Speediest Truck," Argonutz honks.

"You earned that decal," Hercules beeps.

Atalanta beams brightly. She sure did earn it!

ATALANTA

Speed Dash was inspired by myths of Atalanta. Atalanta was a famous Greek heroine and huntress. Stories often tell of her skills as an archer. She once defeated a group of centaurs with her bow. Her arrows helped a group of Greek heroes kill the monstrous Calydonian Boar.

But what Atalanta is most well known for is her quickness. She could outrun anybody.

Atalanta's father said that whoever wanted to marry his daughter had to challenge her to a race. If they won, they could be her husband. If they lost, they would be put to death.

No one could beat Atalanta. But that did not stop the Greek hero Meleager from challenging her.

Meleager had secretly asked for helped from Aphrodite, the goddess of love. She gave him three golden apples.

During the race, Meleager dropped one of the golden apples. Atalanta stopped to look at it, and Meleager took the lead. As Atalanta was about to catch up, he dropped another apple. Again, Atalanta stopped. When she was about to catch up again, Meleager dropped the last apple. Atalanta stopped just long enough so that Meleager could win the race.

BLAKE HOENA

Blake Hoena grew up in central Wisconsin, where he wrote stories about robots conquering the moon and trolls lumbering around the woods behind his parents' house. He now lives in St. Paul, Minnesota, with his two dogs, Ty and Stich. Blake continues to make up stories about things like space aliens and superheroes, and he has written more than 100 chapter books and graphic novels for children.

FERN CANO

Fernando Cano is an illustrator born in Mexico City, Mexico. He currently resides in Monterrey, Mexico, where he works as a free-lance illustrator and concept artist. He has done illustration work for Marvel, DC Comics, and worked on various video game projects in diverse titles. When he's not making art for comics or books, he enjoys hanging out with friends, singing, rowing, and drawing.

GLOSSARY

berm (BURM) – a shoulder or ledge along a road or canal

boulder (BOHL-dur) – a large rounded rock

cavern (KA-vuhrn) – a deep hollow place underground

congratulate (kuhn-GRA-chew-layt) – to tell someone that you are pleased because they have done something well

monstrous (MON-struss) – large and frightening

sliver (SLIV-ur) — a very thin piece of something

straightaways (STRAYT-uh-way) – long, straight parts of a track

MORE MONSTER MYTHS

ONLY FROM

CAPSTONE